PZ
8.3
.L546
S6
1987

17.1
0895460

003509848

P9-CDU-947

PZ8.3.L546S6 1987   A089546001

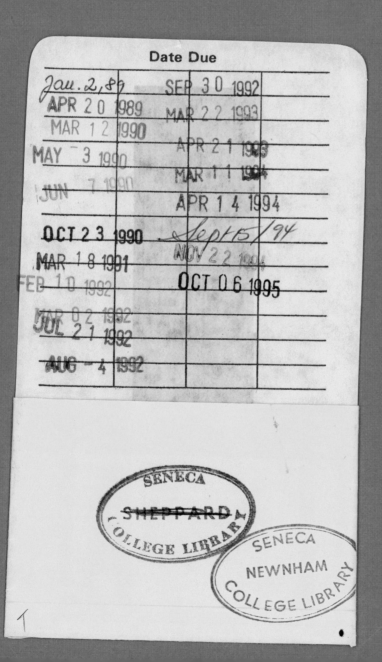

Date Due

Jan. 2, 89	SEP 30 1992
APR 20 1989	MAR 22 1993
MAR 12 1990	APR 21 1993
MAY 3 1990	MAR 11 1994
JUN 7 1990	APR 14 1994
OCT 23 1990	Sept 15/94
MAR 18 1991	NOV 22 1994
FEB 10 1992	OCT 06 1995
MAR 02 1992	
JUL 21 1992	
AUG 4 1992	

SENECA SHEPPARD COLLEGE LIBRARY

SENECA NEWNHAM COLLEGE LIBRARY

Sing a Song of People

by Lois Lenski

Illustrated by Giles Laroche

Little, Brown and Company
Boston   Toronto

1714235 90
RECEIVED NOV 1 1985
SENECA
SHEPPARD
COLLEGE LIBRARY

Illustrations Copyright © 1987 by Giles Laroche
Text Copyright © 1965 by The Lois Lenski Covey Foundation, Inc.
All rights reserved. No part of this book may be reproduced in any form or
by any electronic or mechanical means, including information storage and
retrieval systems, without permission in writing from the publisher, except
by a reviewer who may quote brief passages in a review.

First Edition

The text of "Sing a Song of People" first appeared in *The Life I Live* by Lois
Lenski, and is reprinted here by arrangement with The Lois Lenski Covey
Foundation, Inc.

Library of Congress Cataloging-in-Publication Data
Lenski, Lois, 1893–
   Sing a song of people.

   Summary: Depicts the pleasures of city life, people alone and in crowds,
smiling and hurrying, on the sidewalk, bus, and subway.
   [1. City and town life—Fiction. 2. Stories in
rhyme] I. Laroche, Giles, ill. II. Title.
PZ8.3.L546Si 1987   [E]   86-20873
ISBN 0–316–52074–8
  10   9   8   7   6   5   4   3   2

Designed by Trisha Hanlon
WOR
*Published simultaneously in Canada
by Little, Brown & Company (Canada) Limited*

Printed in the United States of America

For Andrea and Beth

Sing a song of people
Walking fast or slow;

People in the city,
Up and down they go.

People on the sidewalk,

People on the bus;

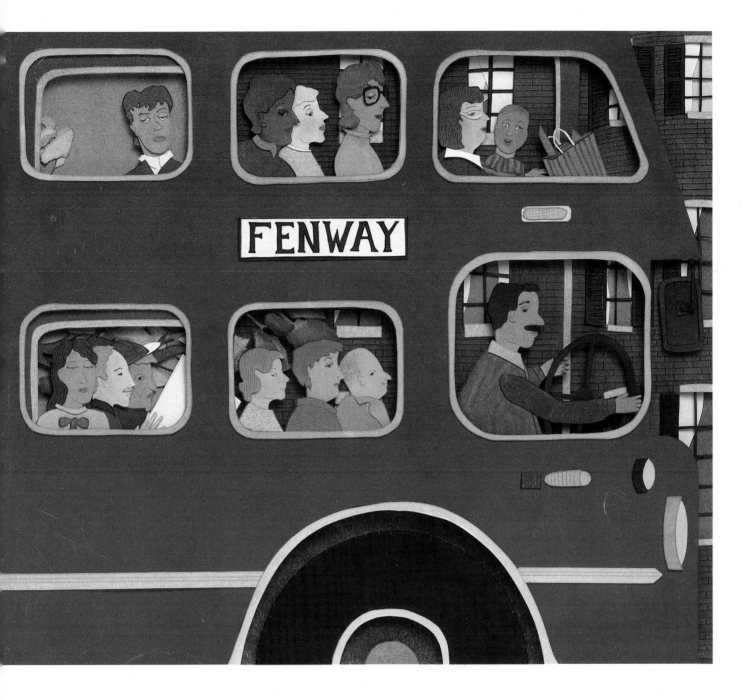

People passing, passing,

In back and front of us.

People on the subway
Underneath the ground;

People riding taxis
Round and round and round.

People with their hats on,

Going in the doors;

People with umbrellas
When it rains and pours.

People in tall buildings

And in stores below;

Riding in elevators
Up and down they go.

People walking singly,

People in a crowd;

People saying nothing,
People talking loud.

People laughing, smiling,

Grumpy people too;

People who just hurry
And never look at you!

Sing a song of people
Who like to come and go;

Sing of city people
You see but never know!